TAPICERO
TAP TAP

Tundra Books

Published in Canada by Tundra Books,
75 Sherbourne Street, Toronto, Ontario M5A 2P9

Published in the United States by Tundra Books of
Northern New York,
P.O. Box 1030, Plattsburgh, New York 12901

Library of Congress Control Number: 2005927014

Library and Archives Canada Cataloguing in Publication

Aska, Warabé
    Tapicero Tap Tap / Warabé Aska.

ISBN 0-88776-760-5

    I. Title.

PS8551.S55T36 2006   jC13'.54   C2005-903340-1

We acknowledge the financial support of the Government of
Canada through the Book Publishing Industry Development
Program (BPIDP) and that of the Government of Ontario
through the Ontario Media Development Corporation's Ontario
Book Initiative. We further acknowledge the support of the
Canada Council for the Arts and the Ontario Arts Council for
our publishing program.

ONTARIO ARTS COUNCIL
CONSEIL DES ARTS DE L'ONTARIO

Medium: Oil on canvas

Printed in China

1 2 3 4 5 6   11 10 09 08 07 06

For my family and friends, who have big dreams.

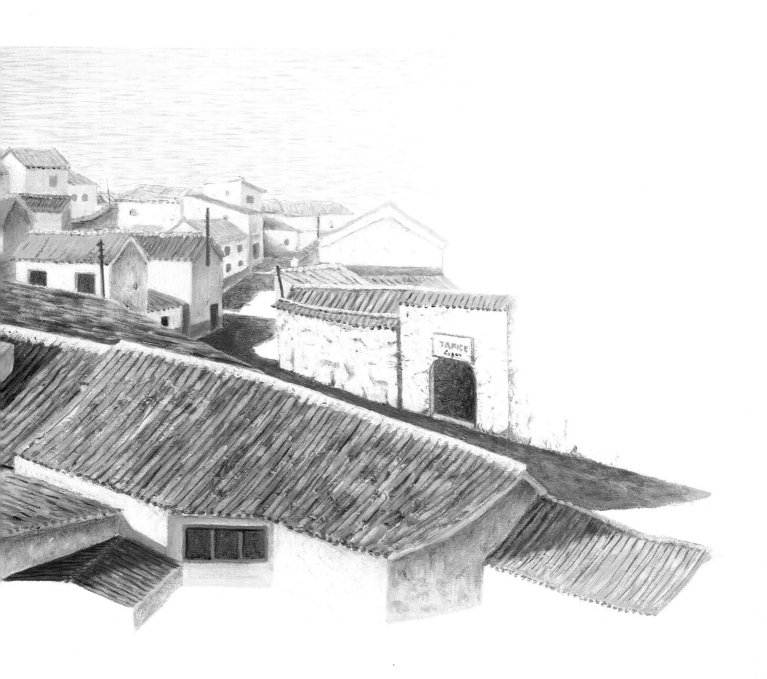

In a sleepy Spanish town by the sea, Tapicero Tap Tap draws open the heavy oak door to his workshop every morning. Inside, the cool dark air smells of clean wood. All day I hear his hammer *tap tap tap* as he makes sofas and chairs.

Tapicero Tap Tap seldom leaves his village by the sea, but once he had dreams. Big dreams. I know, because he is my grandpapa and he told me.

One afternoon during siesta, when it was too hot to sleep, I said, "Rest, Mama. I can take care of Pedrito."

"Are you sure? Your little brother is a handful," Mama replied, but she sounded grateful. "I will put my feet up while the baby naps."

"Take me to the sea!" Pedrito whined.

"It's too hot to be on the sand," I said.

"But there is nothing to do here. No one wants to play with me."

The summer sun made him cranky. I was afraid that he would wake the baby.

Grandpapa was in his workshop, building a giant sofa for the fiesta.

"I know," I said, "follow me! Maybe Grandpapa can help."

"Aw, he's too old." Pedrito rubbed his eyes with his fists.

When Grandpapa saw us in the doorway, the *tap tap tap* of his hammer stopped.

"I wasn't always old, you know," he said. Pedrito looked at him doubtfully. Laying aside his tools, Grandpapa continued, "I'll tell you what. Bring your friends up the hill, where there is a breeze, and I will tell you a story."

And that is what we did. Tapicero Tap Tap's stories are as fine as his furniture.

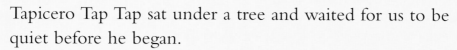

Tapicero Tap Tap sat under a tree and waited for us to be quiet before he began.

"When I was a boy, not much older than you, I would go down to the shore where the fishermen talked of far-off places and tastes that dazzled the tongue and customs strange and beautiful to behold. I wanted to sail across the ocean to see what I could see. How I wanted to taste what they had tasted and see what they had seen and meet the people they had met! Those were my dreams."

"And did they come true?" I said.

"You decide" was his answer.

Tapicero Tap Tap plucked a piece of grass and rubbed it between his fingers. "When I was young, the world was whole. My first memories are of my dear mama taking me to the park. Oh, it was fine in those days before the war. The women gathered flowers in woven baskets to decorate their tables.

"When I was older, we would play in the sand, my friends and I, and I would think about what lay beyond the ocean and how, one day, I would see what I could see.

"Then came the war and, with it, hard times. Everything changed in our town. There was little to eat and the sounds were of bullets and cannons firing. Papa did not come home from the war. I stayed where I was and made furniture, as there was little money for travel.

"The years have gone by and still I make furniture."
   "But that's so sad!" I cried.
   "Is it?"
   "What about the tastes you wanted to try and the customs
you wanted to see and the people you wanted to meet?"

"I learned to relish the tastes of home," said Grandpapa.
"We grow fine grapes here, you know, and we make fine
wine. And we have our own customs."

"Like the fiesta!" said Pedrito.

"Yes. The fiesta. One year they made me the leader of our group in the costume parade competition. My grandpapa gave me a splendid idea for costumes. We sewed horns on jute bags and painted bulls on the bags."

I knew Pedrito was thinking about our grandpapa having a grandpapa of his own.

"What a wonder! Our bullfight was the best part of the parade and we won first prize. I was treated like a hero. My dear grandpapa was so proud."

Tapicero Tap Tap paused. "That was when I knew the pleasure in creating something that people would enjoy. Now I make chairs that hold people while they have a good dinner, or when they read a book about the vast heavens, or when they have visitors from far away.

"*Viva fiesta!* Before long it will be fiesta time again. I always
wanted to meet people from far away and, at fiesta time, I do.

"I still go down to the shore where the fishermen talk of far-off places and tastes that dazzle the tongue and customs strange and beautiful to behold. Do you think my dreams came true?"

The cicadas shrieked and I could hear the *lap lap lap* of the sea on the shore below us.

Finally, Tapicero Tap Tap spoke again. "I have tasted the tastes that dazzle the tongue, and I've seen customs strange and beautiful. And, best of all, I have met a great many people from far away. My story is a happy one." He rose up. "Now it's time to go back to my workshop. I must finish the fiesta sofa and I have little time."

"Why, Grandpapa?" asked Pedrito.

"Because, next week, I am going to sail across the ocean to see what I can see and, when I have seen it, I shall return."

With nightfall, the air turned cooler. Mama put Pedrito and the baby to bed. As I lay under my covers, I could hear the *tap tap tap* of Grandpapa's hammer.